NOAH

Patricia Lee Gauch

illustrated by Jonathan Green

Penguin Putnam Books for Young Readers

Here is

NOAH

with grace in his eyes,

Here are his sons
right by his side.
But the people on earth
are not good at all.

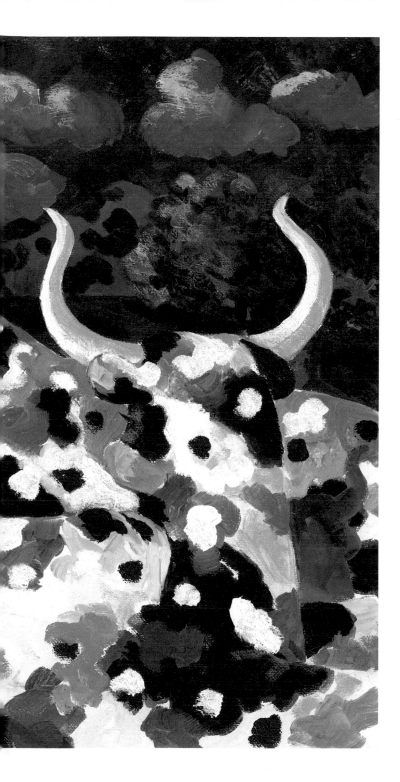

"Build an ark,"
said God to Noah,
"with a window,
with a door,
with three stories tall.
Build an ark," said God to Noah,
"because it's going to rain
and rain and rain.
Then take your wife,
take your sons,
and their wives, too.
Take creatures that crawl
and birds that fly,
animals tall and animals small,
take all kinds of animals,
two by two,"
said God to Noah.

And that is what Noah did.

He built with beams
and he built with nails.
He built in a window,
and he built in a door,
and the ark grew wide
and the ark grew tall,
big enough for all the animals,
    two by two.

Then Noah called them,
birds that flew,
robins, sparrows,
crows and vultures,
cockatoos, parrots, tanagers, and ibises.
He called every kind of bird,
   two by two.

And he called creeping things,
snakes and lizards,
tortoises and turtles,
crocodiles, salamanders, alligators, too.
Every kind of creeping thing,
     two by two.

Then he called to the fields
and he called to the hills:
"MICE AND GOPHERS!
ANTELOPES AND ELEPHANTS!
GIRAFFES, ZEBRAS,
RHINO-RHINOCEROSES,
EVERY KIND OF ANIMAL, COME,
     two by two!"

And then it started to rain.
One day, two days, three days,
four, five days, six days
and seven days more.
It rained for forty days
and forty more nights.
And the animals huddled,
    two by two.

It rained and it rained,
rained and rained.
But safe inside were
Noah and his wife
and his sons and their wives
and all of the animals,
two by two.

Now the waters rose
and they covered the earth
and the ark it floated on top.
And still it rained,
one day, two days, three days,
four, five days, six days,
seven days more.
For one hundred days
and fifty days more,
it rained and rained,
rained and rained.

Then a light wind blew
and the sun came out,
and the rain
    stopped.

And Noah saw a mountain,
and then he saw more,
and he opened up his window
and he sent forth a raven,
who flew and flew,
and found only
        water.
So Noah sent a dove
out across the water,
and it flew and it flew,
flew and flew.
Finally the dove found
        land,
and it brought back
        an olive leaf.
Noah was
        happy.

And soon as soon,
out came the sun,
and the waters went away,
and the earth dried up,
and God said, "It's time,"
and Noah said, "It's time,"
and he opened up the windows
and he opened up the doors,
and he said to the animals,
"Go back to your fields,
go back to your mountains,
go back to your ponds. Go,
        two by two."

And off went the robins, sparrows,
crows and vultures,
cockatoos, parrots, tanagers, ibises.
Snakes and lizards,
tortoises and turtles,
crocodiles, salamanders, alligators, too.
Mice and gophers,
antelopes and elephants,
giraffes, zebras, rhino-rhinoceroses,
all of the animals went,
    two by two.